If Peas Could Taste Like Candy

Other Books by Crystal Bowman

Cracks in the Sidewalk
Ivan and the Dynamos
Jonathan James Says, "Christmas Is Coming!"
Jonathan James Says, "Happy Birthday to Me!"
Jonathan James Says, "I Can Be Brave!"
Jonathan James Says, "I Can Hardly Wait!"
Jonathan James Says, "I Can Help!"
Jonathan James Says, "Let's Be Friends!"
Jonathan James Says, "Let's Play Ball!"
Jonathan James Says, "School's Out!"

If Peas Could Taste Like Candy

and Other Funny Poems for Kids

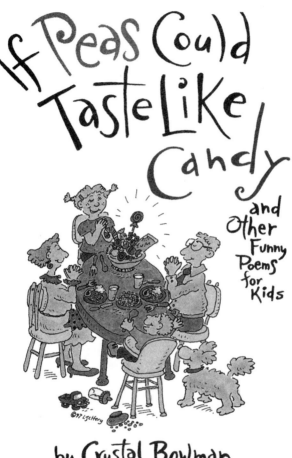

by Crystal Bowman

illustrated by Lynn Jeffery

ZondervanPublishingHouse

Grand Rapids, Michigan

A Division of HarperCollinsPublishers

If Peas Could Taste Like Candy
Text copyright © 1998 by Crystal Bowman
Illustrations copyright © 1998 by Lynn Jeffery

Requests for information should be addressed to:

 ZondervanPublishingHouse
Grand Rapids, Michigan 49530

Library of Congress Cataloging-in-Publication Data

Bowman, Crystal.
    If peas could taste like candy and other funny poems for kids / by Crystal
Bowman; illustrated by Lynn Jeffery.
        p.   cm.
    Summary: A collection of humorous poems about school, love, church, families,
and God.
    ISBN: 0-310-21950-7 (hardcover)
    1.Children's poetry, American.   2. Humorous poetry, American.
[1. Humorous poety. 2. American poetry.] I. Jeffery, Lynn, ill. II. Title.
PS3552.087563I4   1998
811'.54—dc21   97-40082
                                                          CIP
                                                           AC

This edition printed on acid-free paper and meets the American National Standards
Institute Z39.48 standard.

Printed in the United States of America

98 99 00 01 02 03 /❖ DC/ 10 9 8 7 6 5 4 3 2

To David and Julie

Special thanks to my editors,
Lori Walburg and Sue Hill

IF PEAS COULD TASTE LIKE CANDY

Dear God, please bless this dinner
That we're about to eat.
And with your special blessing,
Please make the food taste sweet.

If peas could taste like candy,
And fish like chocolate pie,
Then I'd gladly eat my dinner.
So please, God, could you try?

If my milk could taste like Kool-Aid,
Dear God, I know you're able,
It'd make me very thankful
For the food that's on the table.

If you could add some sugar,
I don't think that would hurt.
'Cause if I eat my dinner,
I get to have dessert.

FRIENDS

A friend is someone who listens,
A friend is someone who cares.
A friend is someone who understands,
A friend is someone who shares.

It's nice to have a special friend
To tell all your secrets to.
It's nice to know that someone you like,
Is someone who really likes you.

A friend is someone you call on the phone
To talk about nothing at all.
A friend is someone who cheers you up
And makes you feel ten feet tall.

Everyone would like to have
A special friend, it's true.
But if you want a special friend,
You need to be one, too.

STOMACHACHE

Oh, why do I have a stomachache?
All I had was some chocolate cake,
A double-nutty candy bar,
And jelly beans
From Grandpa's jar,
An ice-cream cone
With sprinkles on top,
A super jumbo lollipop,
A cookie
And some bubble gum—
A stomachache is not much fun!
It hurts so bad I think I'll cry.
But still I have to wonder
WHY?

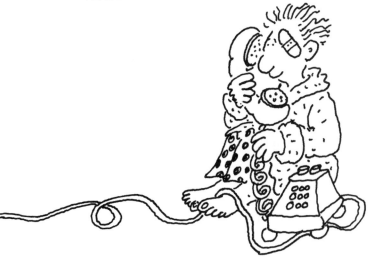

A SOLID HOUSE AND A LITTLE MOUSE

Once there was a foolish man
Who built his house upon the sand.
He made it out of stone and brick,
And mortar that would make it stick.

And in the corner of the house,
There lived a cozy little mouse.

But one day, when the rain came down,
The house went tumbling to the ground.
It could not last, it could not stand—
For it was built upon the sand.

And then that cozy little mouse,
Set out to find another house.

There was a wiser man one day,
Who built his house the very same way.
But on a rock his house was built,
Not on a ground of sand and silt.

And so that cozy little mouse
Made his home in this man's house.

Now every time the rain came down,
This man's house was safe and sound.
The house stood firm; it did not fall.
It did not shake, no not at all.

And in the corner of the house,
Slept the cozy little mouse.

Now even though this story's nice—
You may have heard it once or twice,
There's something you must understand
About the rock and rain and sand.

When people do things their own way,
There is a price they'll have to pay.
They're like the house on sandy ground—
When problems come, they'll tumble down.

But if we do things Jesus' way,
And listen to him every day,
Our lives will be so safe and sound,
Just like the house on solid ground.

The Bible tells us what to do,
And Jesus' words are always true.
And if you're in a solid house,
You'll be as cozy as the mouse!

ALONE AT THE PLAYGROUND

I rode my bike to the playground,
But nobody else was there.
I had to play all by myself,
But I didn't really care.

I zipped and slipped down the twisty slide
A billion, zillion times—
No pushin' and no shovin'
And no fightin' in the lines.

I climbed to the top of the monkey bars,
I shouted and screamed out loud,
"Hey! I'm king of the jungle gym!"
I couldn't do that in a crowd!

I played by myself in the sandbox—
Didn't have to share the toys
With selfish, screamin', cryin',
Sissy girls and bully boys.

All by myself at the playground
Was delightfully entertaining,
Even though I got soaking wet—
Did I mention it was raining?

I DON'T LIKE

I don't like doing fractions.
I don't like doing chores.
I hate to do my spelling
When I'd rather play outdoors.

I don't like peas or broccoli.
I don't like writing letters.
I don't like taking bubble baths,
Or wearing itchy sweaters.

I don't like washing dishes.
I don't like pouring rain.
But what I *really* like to do
Is sit here and complain!

THE SNAIL

The snail takes her house
Wherever she goes.
No wonder she goes so slowly.
All you can see are her little toes.
No wonder she goes so slowly.

If she's buried deep beneath the sand,
Or plodding along on top of dry land,
She travels along just as fast as she can—
But she always goes
                    so ...
                            very ...
                                    slowly!

CENTIPEDE

I marvel at the centipede
Who travels at tremendous speed.
I wonder how he seems to know
Where each leg's supposed to go.
It could be harmful to his health
If he should step upon himself!

DAVID AND GOLIATH

Goliath was a bully.
He taunted and he teased,
"Send someone out to fight me—
Send anyone you please!"
The Israelites were frightened.
They didn't want to fight
This giant who was big and mean,
And known for strength and might!

Goliath roared, but they ignored
His deadly invitation.
Then David who was just a boy
With bold determination
Said, "I will fight the giant,
But I don't need a sword,
A shield or suit of armor,
Because I have the Lord."

David found a few small stones
Lying on the ground.
He put one in his slingshot
And he whirled it 'round and 'round.
The stone went soaring through the air
And bonged the giant's head.
Crash! Bang! Goliath fell down.
The mighty giant was dead.

This story goes to show you
That when God is on your side,
Though you may be a little kid,
You're very big inside!

COME OUT

Come out! Come out!
Come out of your shell.
What's wrong, my pet?
Aren't you feeling well?

We can go walking
Down by the sea,
Laughing and talking,
Just you and me.

PLEASE come out,
Come out of your shell.
He won't come out.

Oh, well.

THE FISHERMAN AND
THE WORM

Sometimes the fisherman
catches the fish.
Sometimes the fish
gets the worm.
This little sport of give-and-take
is easy to confirm.

It doesn't take a referee
to know who is the winner.
The champion, of course,
is whoever gets his dinner!

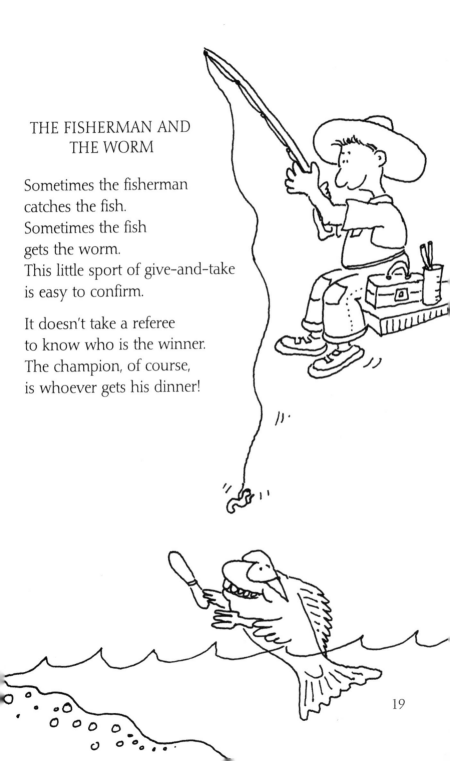

19

DIGGING IN THE TRASH

I'm poking through the slimy garbage,
Digging in the trash.
This smelly, sticky rubbish
Is giving me a rash.

This trash is so disgusting!
I hope I'll soon be done.
Searching through a garbage can
Is really not much fun.

I need to be more careful.
I guess it's not my day.
My retainer isn't something that
I should have thrown away!

BUSY

Sour suckers make me pucker,
Sunshine makes me smile.
When my friends call on the phone
I talk for quite a while.

I use my nose to smell a rose,
I sniff and sneeze and blow.
And with my eyes I read and blink
And look which way to go.

I use my ears to help me hear,
I use my teeth to chew.
My brain is very helpful
'Cause it tells me what to do.

I learn and think, I take a drink,
I whistle and I sing.
I study birds and flowers,
And I find amazing things.

I frown and pout, I sometimes shout,
I laugh till I am dizzy.
And all this makes me realize
My head is very busy!

MY MOTHER'S SICK IN BED

My mother's rather sick in bed.
I'm not the kind to boast,
But I got up and made her
Some coffee, eggs, and toast.

I washed the dirty laundry—
Though it was hard to do.
I really helped my mother,
Who suffered with the flu.

I scrubbed the dishes and the floor,
I cleaned the toilets too.
I polished all the furniture
Until it shined like new.

I cooked some macaroni,
And washed my little brother.
It really is a special joy,
Helping out my mother.

COOL KIDS

Kids who think they're really cool
Are sometimes mean and often cruel.
They pick on you and call you names,
And ruin all the playground games.
They say things that can make you mad,
And they don't care if you are sad.

They act like this most every day—
But I know why they act this way.
Even though they think they're cool,
And act so tough when they're at school,
They really are afraid, you see,
Of other kids like you and me.

That is why they put you down,
And try to boss you all around.
They really don't want you to know
The feelings that they never show.
They're jealous of the things you do.
They know they're not as good as you.

Yes, that is why they act so mean,
And always cause an ugly scene.
So stand up straight and stand up tall.
Don't let them bother you at all.
If you're a kid that's nice at school,
Then *you're* the one who's really cool!

DONNA TOMMA

My name is, Donna Tomma,
and I love, to use, the comma.
I put it where, it doesn't need, to go.
I just love, this punctuation,
it's my new, infatuation,
if I could, I'd put it, right between,
my toes!

MY LITTLE PET RHINOCEROS

I have a pet rhinoceros
Who likes to ride the city bus.
He always causes such a fuss,
My little pet rhinoceros.

One day when he came through the door,
The ladies fainted on the floor.
The children screamed and yelled for more,
They loved my pet rhinoceros.

As we went riding through the town,
The kids were jumping up and down.
The driver thought he was a clown,
My little pet rhinoceros.

A man got on who had a gun.
He started robbing everyone.
No one thought that this was fun,
Except my pet rhinoceros.

He gave a loud enormous roar.
The man went running out the door,
And no one sees him anymore,
Thanks to my rhinoceros.

Reporters came and made a fuss.
He felt so brave and glamorous.
And now he drives the city bus,
My little pet rhinoceros.

IF YOU WANT TO TALK TO GOD

If you want to talk to God,
You'll always find him there,
To listen to your problem,
Your question, or your prayer.

You never have to stand in line
Or come another day.
He is not too busy
To hear you when you pray.

Even though it is his job
To rule the universe,
When you want to talk to him,
You are always first.

He never takes vacations,
He doesn't take a nap.
When you talk to God
It's like sitting in his lap.

If it's morning or it's nighttime
Or somewhere in between,
You never get a busy-buzz
Or answering machine.

He cares about your problems,
Gigantic ones or small.
So if you want to talk to God,
Just give him
A call.

ELEVATOR RIDE

I was on the elevator,
When suddenly it quit.
The doors did not slide open.
I nearly had a fit!

I quickly called for help
On the elevator phone.
It seemed like several hours
That I stood there all alone.

My hands were getting sweaty,
My heart began to race.
I felt a little panicky
Confined to such a space.

I started getting hungry.
I thought I'd die of thirst.
I'd had a few disasters,
But this one was the worst!

I finally heard some voices,
Some people rescued me.
The fact that I was shaken up
Was very plain to see.

"What day is it?" I asked of them.
Then they began to laugh.
They told me I was trapped inside—
Three minutes and a half!

GOD BLESS GRANDMA

Grandma gives me candy,
And she takes me to the zoo.
Grandma bakes me cookies,
And she reads me stories, too.

Grandma doesn't get upset
Each time I make a mess.
And when I ask for something,
She always answers yes!

She listens to my problems,
And she thinks I'm really smart.
I'm glad that God made Grandma
With a kind and loving heart.

So God, please bless my grandma,
And keep her safe and strong.
And God, if it's all right with you,
Please let her live real long.

31

I HAVE NEVER BEEN A MONKEY

I have never been a monkey,
An ape, or chimpanzee.
I have never had a long and hairy
Tail attached to me.

I have never swung from trees,
Though I've climbed one once or twice.
I'm a living human being
And I think it's rather nice.

I can laugh when things are funny,
I can run and jump and walk.
I can read and I can spell,
I can whisper, shout, and talk.

I can sing and I can whistle.
I can even blow my nose.
I am talented and special
From my head down to my toes.

I've been made in God's own image
So it's very plain to see,
That I've never been a monkey,
An ape, or chimpanzee.

ANTS IN MY PANTS

When I opened up my closet door
to find some clothes to wear,
I was certainly astonished
at the creatures that were there.

There were:

    ants in my pants,
    a fox in my socks,
    emus in my shoes,
    a mouse in my blouse,
    sardines in my jeans,
    a bat in my hat,
    and a kitten in my mitten!

They were singing,
they were dancing—
it was quite a grand affair.
So I closed my closet door
and just wore my underwear!

DEAR MOTHER

"Mother!
I don't want to bother you,
but I'm up here in bed
with a cold and the flu.
I don't like being up here
all alone,
so could you bring me
the telephone?
My favorite show is on TV,
so could you turn it on for me?
I need some tissues
in case I sneeze.
And may I have
a magazine, please?
Will you come here
and rub my back?
And bring me popcorn for a snack?
I'd also like
my toenail clippers,
my bathrobe, and my furry slippers.
Mother, dear Mother,
please do as I say."
My dear mother heard me
and came right away.
She looked in my throat and felt my head.
"Get up and get dressed," my mother said.
"Your cold is all better, your forehead is cool,
so grab your books, dear—
you're going to school!"

SUNDAY MORNING

Sunday morning at our house
Is certainly amusing!
We're always in a panic
And it sometimes gets confusing.

My sister hogs the bathroom,
My mom can't find her shoes.
For breakfast I have cereal—
I don't know which to choose.

I have to sort my socks
From the pile in the dryer.
My brother struggles with his tie—
He's singing in the choir.

Our poodle needs to go outside,
The kitten runs away.
We should have started getting ready
Sometime yesterday.

My dad can't find the car keys
So we do a frantic search,
And we're terribly exhausted
When we finally get to church!

HABAKKUK

Habakkuk …
Habakkuk …
That is where I'm always stuck!
These books I need to memorize
So I can earn a special prize.

Esther, Job, Psalms, and Proverbs,
Those I've learned with ease.
But when I get to Habakkuk,
It seems I always freeze.

Habakkuk …
Habakkuk …
Once again, it's where I'm stuck.
I've finally come to realize,
I might not earn a special prize.

KILLER MOSQUITO

They say a killer mosquito
Is coming to our town.
They say that we should lock our doors
And keep our windows down.

They say it's big and ugly,
And it has enormous eyes.
But I can't help but wonder
If it's just a bunch of lies.

They say that its proboscis
Is long and sharp and wide.
They say we must be careful
And that kids should stay inside.

They say it's coming very soon.
I don't believe it's true.

Yes, I'm certain it's a rumor—
Hey, kid! What's wrong with you?

IF YOU EVER MEET A PORCUPINE

If you ever meet a porcupine
   be careful not to pet it.
'Cause if you pet a porcupine
   you surely will regret it!

MIDDLE CHILD

My life is not too pleasant
since I'm the middle child.
My siblings have a tendency
to get me very riled.

My older brother thinks that he's
the most important one.
And everything I try to do
he has already done.

My younger sister gets her way,
I guess because she's little.
But me—I'm nothing special,
I am stuck right in the
middle.

My closet's full of hand-me-downs;
my sister breaks my toys.
I don't have any privacy;
there's always too much noise.

Yes, being in the middle
is distressing there's no doubt—
except when I do homework
and my brother helps me out.

And when I'm playing basketball
it's much more fun with two.
Without my older brother,
I don't know what I'd do.

At times when I am feeling sad
my sister makes me smile.
I guess it's really not so bad
when you're the
middle
child!

THE WATCH

I found a super-duper watch.
It has a leather band.
It tells the days and hours,
And it has a second hand.

It has a little buzzer
And a nifty-neat alarm.
It fits me just exactly
When I strap it on my arm.

It even has a tiny light
That twinkles in the dark.
I found the watch the other day
While playing at the park.

I can't believe I found it.
This watch is really fine—
The greatest watch I've ever seen.
Too bad it isn't mine!

THE HAPPY HIPPOPOTAMUS

I know a hippopotamus
Who always wears a smile.
He wallows in the water
And is happy all the while.
The elephants and tigers
Come visit him each day.
They tell him jungle stories
Before they go their way.

The birds all come from miles around
To sing a cheerful song.
They love the happy hippo's smile,
And stay the whole day long.
The antelopes and zebras
Come to see him, too.
The happy hippopotamus
Is never sad or blue.

So if you want a lot of friends
To visit you each day,
Just wear a happy smile,
And watch them come your way.

I DIDN'T KNOW

I didn't know
I was supposed to go
To the store to help my mother.

I didn't know
I was supposed to show
The mail to my older brother.

I didn't know
I was supposed to mow
The lawn this afternoon.

I didn't know
I was supposed to throw
The trash away so soon.

I didn't know
I was supposed to go slow
When doing my addition.

But that's what happens,
Now I know,
When I forget to listen.

I CAN'T FIND MY GLASSES

I can't find my glasses,
Oh, where can they be?
I looked on my desk,
And beside the TV.
I looked in my backpack
And under my chair.
I looked on the table,
But they were not there.

I looked on my dresser
And searched every drawer.
They weren't on my nightstand,
They weren't on the floor.
I looked for my glasses
All over the place.
I finally found them
Right on
My face!

PING-PONG

Ping-Pong, ka-ping, ka-pong.
Whip, smack!
Hit it back.

Ping-Pong, ka-ping, ka-pong.
Power serve—
Watch it curve.

Ping-Pong, ka-ping, ka-pong.
Over the net,
You bet!

Ping-Pong, ka-ping, ka-pong.
Too much fun!
Twenty-one,
Game is done.
I won!

THE CIRCLE POEM

Writing a poem in a circle is an interesting thing to do. But it makes me rather dizzy, and it's kind of hard to read, too. I just thought I would try it — it's a challenge, I admit. But now I'm in the center, and so I'm going to quit!

PHILLIP PHENNY PHAN

"The letter *F* should not exist!"
Phillip Phenny Phan insists—
A phine phantastic phellow
Phull of charm.
As he walks his phather's dogs,
And he phollows phrisky phrogs,
He enjoys the phragrant phlowers
On the pharm.

He phiddles by the phire,
He's a tenor in the choir,
And he serenades his mother
With the phlute.
He is witty, he is phun,
He enjoys a silly pun,
And his phavorite phood
Is phancy phrozen phruit.

"I am not a phoolish man,"
Says Phillip Phenny Phan,
"I just don't like
Unnecessary stuphph.
The *F*'s a phlaky letter,
But the *P* and *H* are better—
So twenty-phive good letters
Are enough!"

I'M NOT AFRAID

I'm not afraid of spiders,
I'm not afraid of frogs.
I'm not afraid of buzzing bees,
Or even barking dogs.

I'm not afraid of monsters,
I'm not afraid of sharks.
I'm not afraid to be alone,
Not even when it's dark.

I'm not afraid of thunderstorms,
Or very scary books.
I'm not afraid of boogeymen,
Or mean old Captain Hook.

I'm brave and I'm courageous,
I've got confidence inside.
Oh, no! Here comes a girl—
I think I'll run and hide!

OUR FATHER'S WORLD

God created the mountains.
He poured out the deep blue sea.
Green fields and rolling meadows
He made for you and me.

He made the singing birds,
The flowers, and the trees;
All the plants and animals,
And even buzzing bees.

God created the sun and moon,
The bright and twinkling stars,
And all the planets out in space
From Jupiter to Mars.

He made a great big universe
Where you and I can play,
Enjoying his creation
Each and every day.

Now it's up to you and me
To keep things fresh and clean,
To take care of the earth and sky
And all things in between.

I know it would be possible
If each one did his part.
At home and in the neighborhood
Are places we can start.

I'll plant a tree, you pick up trash—
It helps a little bit.
Because we love our Father's world,
Let's take good care of it.

DARE

Someone dared me to eat a worm—
   All I can say is yuck!

I dared to kiss the monkey bars—
   My lips got frozen stuck!

Someone dared me to put a tack
upon my teacher's chair—
   I got in lots of trouble,
   because I took the dare.

Someone dared me to walk on the ice—
   My feet got cold and wet.

Someone dared me to start a fight—
   It's something I regret!

I've finally learned my lesson,
   No longer am I a fool.
Taking a dare from someone else
   Is really not that cool!

BEDTIME FRIENDS

I need my monkey and my sheep
To lie beside me while I sleep.
I want my camel and my frog,
My penguin and my cuddly dog.

I can't get by without my cat,
My tiger and my purple rat.
If I don't have my horse it seems
I always get those scary dreams.

I need my favorite teddy bear,
My bunny with its furry hair,
My zebra and my unicorn—
Even though their fur is worn.

My duck, my whale, my dinosaur,
My lion with its fearful roar.
I need my fuzzy bumblebee—
Hey! Now there is no room for me!

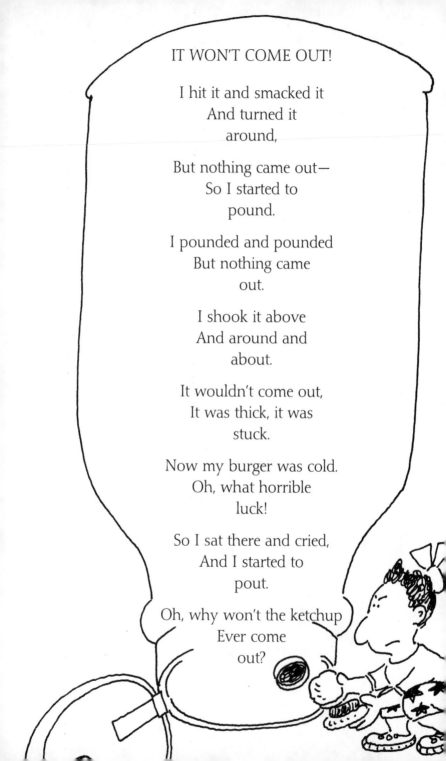

IT WON'T COME OUT!

I hit it and smacked it
And turned it
around,

But nothing came out—
So I started to
pound.

I pounded and pounded
But nothing came
out.

I shook it above
And around and
about.

It wouldn't come out,
It was thick, it was
stuck.

Now my burger was cold.
Oh, what horrible
luck!

So I sat there and cried,
And I started to
pout.

Oh, why won't the ketchup
Ever come
out?

I LIKE TO BE ANNOYING

I like to be annoying.
I like to pinch and squeeze.
I like to play a practical joke.
I like to taunt and tease.

It's so much fun to bother
My sister and my brother.
I love to scare and horrify
My father and my mother.

I like to be annoying—
The excitement never ends.
But I can't help but wonder:
Why don't I have any friends?

TWO LITTLE HAMSTERS

I had two little hamsters,
Then I noticed I had four.
Four little hamsters for me to adore.

Then a few weeks later,
I saw that there were more.
More little hamsters than ever before.

In the bedroom on the floor,
In the bathroom in the drawer.
Hamsters and hamsters and hamsters galore.

Feeding and cleaning became quite a chore.
Mother and Father said,
"THAT'S IT! NO MORE!"

So I gave them away to the lady next door,
To the boy down the street,
And the man at the shore.

I gave them away to my friends at the store,
To the young and the old,
To the rich and the poor.

Out of my house, out through the door.
My hamsters are gone,
Forevermore.

A BAD DAY

I fell out of bed and my cat ran away.
I'm having a miserable, horrible day.

My pants are too short, my hair is a fright.
I'm positive nothing is going to be right.

My socks have holes, I can't find my shoes.
This kind of day really gives me the blues.

My pancakes got burned, the milk is all gone.
Oh, why does everything keep going wrong?

My homework's not done and today there's a quiz.
Oh, it doesn't get any sadder than this.

"School has been canceled," Mom called out to me.
Today is the best that it ever could be!

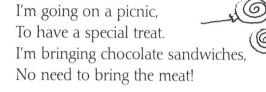

I'M GOING ON A PICNIC

I'm going on a picnic,
To have a special treat.
I'm bringing chocolate sandwiches,
No need to bring the meat!

I've packed some bags of jelly beans,
Some chewy cookies too,
I'm bringing chips and doughnuts,
'Cause healthy food won't do.

I've packed an extra lollipop,
And when I find a friend,
We'll share my bag of goodies,
'Cause this picnic's just pretend!

MARY MARY HUCKLEBERRY

Mary Mary Huckleberry
Loved to read the dictionary.
Even when the sun
Would shine,
Mary read it all the time.

She didn't call her girlfriends,
She never went away.
For she preferred
To learn the words
And didn't want to play.

Her hair grew forty inches,
Her clothes got rather tight,
But Mary looked
Inside the book
Morning, noon, and night.

Her skin turned into wrinkles
As she began to age,
But still her eyes
Were mesmerized
By words upon the page.

Mary Mary Huckleberry
Read the entire dictionary.
Fifty years
Inside her room,
She read the words from A to ZOOM.

"At last I've read the dictionary,"
Mary Mary said.
And with a sigh
She closed her eyes,
And finally went to bed!

LOVE

Love is being thoughtful,
And being kind to others.
Love is being helpful
To your sisters and your brothers.

Love is being patient.
Love is when you share.
Love is doing little things
That show how much you care.

Love is when you listen
To your mother or your dad,
And when you pray for someone
Who is sick or who is sad.

Love is giving food and clothes
To those who don't have much.
Love can be a phone call,
Or a letter or a touch.

Love is just so many things—
It's more than I can mention.
But most of all, God is love,
'Cause it was his invention!

SPRING

It's spring! It's spring!
What a wonderful thing!
The leaves burst out
And the little robins sing.

The ducklings are born;
The grass comes alive.
The bees are busy
Building their hive.

I smell the tulips and daffodils—
Ah-choo! Where are my allergy pills?
Itchy, watery, burning eyes
Watching pretty butterflies.
Sniff, sneeze, cough, and wheeze—
Pass me a box of tissues, please!

It's spring! It's spring!
So run and play—
But I will stay inside today!

DANIEL

Daniel was a fine young man
who prayed three times a day.
But then the king
said a foolish thing:
"To me alone you must pray!
You may not pray to other gods."
So Daniel had to choose—
deny his God,
or break the law.
Either way, he'd lose!

If anyone did not obey
the law that had been passed,
  he'd spend his day
    a different way—
     to the lions he'd be cast.

     But Daniel did not worry.
     He prayed in broad daylight.
     And Daniel then
     was in the den—
     he hoped they wouldn't bite!

The Lord protected Daniel
and shut the lions' jaws.
They didn't roar
like they had before,
or even use their claws.
The king was so astonished
that Daniel was okay.
He got him out
and shouted:
"Daniel's God we will obey!"

I KNOW A KID

I know a kid who picks his nose.
He licks his fingers and his toes.
This kid is also rather rude,
He whines and cries and throws his food.

He likes to scream, he likes to stare,
Don't get too close—he'll pull your hair.
He often likes to suck his thumb
And play with sticky bubble gum.

He likes to bite on fingernails,
And pull on little puppies' tails.
He makes a mess with every sneeze.
He never uses "thanks" or "please."

He likes to burp, he likes to spit,
He sometimes even throws a fit.
I finally went and asked my mother,
"Must we keep this baby brother?"

HUNGRY AS A BEAR

One day when I was playing,
I was hungry as could be.
So I ate a bear and lion,
And I ate a chimpanzee.

Then I ate a cow and zebra
And a camel and a horse.
And when I ate the hippo,
I was very full, of course.

I'm sure you think I'm lying
From my head down to my socks.
But the animals I ate
Were only crackers from a box.

JEHOSHAPHAT

My parents named me Jehoshaphat.
Oh, what on earth can I do?
By the time I learn how to spell it,
I might be one hundred and two!

No one ever pronounces it right,
They always get it wrong.
It really is terribly troublesome
To have a name that's so long.

My friends can't fit Jehoshaphat
On their little valentines.
When I write it on my paper,
It takes up twenty lines.

And when I'm playing baseball
No one ever shouts my name,
Even if I catch the ball
And win the baseball game.

A name is such an important thing,
I could go on and on.
If my parents wanted a Bible name
They could have named me John.

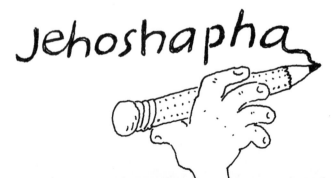

THE CHRISTMAS PLAY

Here I am on center stage
In the Christmas play tonight.
I've memorized my special part—
I hope I get it right!

I've practiced many hours,
I'm very well prepared.
But still I'm feeling nervous,
And just a little scared.

"Hallelujah!" sing the angels,
As they flap their wings and fly.
"Let's hurry to the manger!"
The eager shepherds cry.

Joseph lays the baby
In his tiny little bed.
Mary whispers softly
As she pats him on the head.

My heart is beating faster,
I know this is my cue—
"Baa, baa, baa," I say,
For I'm a little ewe.

MY TEACHER

My teacher's strict, my teacher's mean,
I don't like her at all.
She made me wash the blackboard
And hang pictures on the wall.

I just don't think she likes me,
She makes me sit so still.
She makes me listen all day long
And that's against my will.

Yesterday she made me take
A boring spelling test.
She gave it back, I got an A.
My teacher is the best!

ME FIRST

I want to go first!
I want to go first!
I'm so excited
I think I will burst!

Me first!
Me first!
Being last is always the worst!
Please, please let me go first!

What? What's that you say?
We're getting our shots today?
Okay—*you* can go first.

JOHN LIKES BUGS

John likes bugs in science class,
Sarah plays the flute.
Michael is the best there is
At Trivial Pursuit.

Matt likes kicking soccer balls,
Joey likes to run.
Kelly thinks that basketball's
The best way to have fun.

Lori likes arithmetic.
Kim knows how to rhyme.
Jason loves to paint and draw—
He does it all the time.

Lee knows all the planets
Like Jupiter and Mars.
Sue likes swinging upside down,
Beneath the monkey bars.

Charlie is a hockey fan,
Jamie likes to sing.
Sherri goes to dancing class,
'Cause that's her favorite thing.

Yes, life is full of many things
For children to enjoy,
And everyone is quite unique,
Every girl and boy.

So whether you like bugs or art
Or playing basketball,
Doing what *you* like to do—
Is the very best thing of all.

THE OFFERING

The offering plate was passed to me,
I quietly put in my money.
But by mistake my gum fell in—
It wasn't very funny.

I tried to get my bubble gum back,
But it was way too late.
The person sitting next to me
Had passed the offering plate.

I didn't have more bubble gum
So I was feeling blue.
'Twas double juicy jungle fruit,
My favorite gum to chew.

My gum is gone forever.
I must not moan or whine.
But if the preacher gets it,
I hope he likes that kind!

PAPA'S PIZZA

Welcome to Papa's Pizza Place.
Our sauce is from a tomato base.
We've fourteen toppings to be precise,
They're all included in the price:

Italian ants and garlic bees,
Romano worms and ricotta fleas,
Parmesan beetles, red pepper bugs,
Alfredo roaches, oregano slugs,
mushrooms stuffed with lizard tails,
spicy marinara snails,
olive oil pollywogs,
tasty mozzarella frogs,
onion moths and pepperoni ticks,
I'm sure you'll love our Italian mix!

I walked away and shook my head.
I went next door,
For a taco instead!

MY INVISIBLE ELEPHANT

I have an invisible elephant
Who comes with me to school.
He's proper and obedient—
He follows every rule.

I play with him at recess—
He makes a splendid slide.
I climb on his enormous back,
He takes me for a ride.

Whenever I play basketball,
He lifts me with his trunk.
My friends are all astounded
At the way that I can dunk!

He teaches me my spelling words,
He helps me with subtraction.
He's very kind and gentle,
And he's never a distraction.

I'm glad that he's invisible
and no one knows he's there.
But how on earth do I explain
About that broken chair?

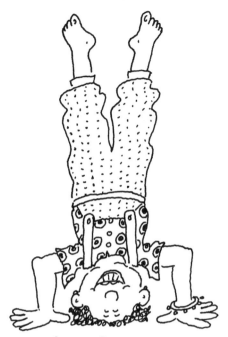

UPSIDE-DOWN POEM

I'm writing this poem upside down
While standing on my head.
My feet are getting tingly
And my face is turning red.

It's kind of hard to write
When my body's upside down.
My head is feeling heavy
And the room is turned around.

I'd better finish quickly
To make this poem complete,
'Cause my head will feel much better
When I'm standing on my feet.

NO KIDS ALLOWED!

"No kids allowed!
No kids allowed!"
That's what the grown-ups say.
We can't go here.
We can't go there.
It happens every day.

"You're much too young!
You're much too small!"
That's what we're always told.
So is it any wonder
We can't wait till we are old?

MY HIDING PLACE

I have a secret hiding place,
It's right inside my home.
It's the place I always go to
When I want to be alone.

It is very warm and cozy,
And it even has a light.
Sometimes I stay for hours—
I can even spend the night.

It's a great place to escape
When my sister gets annoying.
And no one is aware of
All the things that I'm enjoying.

I can read my favorite story,
Or recite a silly poem.
I can even sit and think—
It's my home inside my home.

It always comes in handy
When I'm feeling sad and blue.
It's the closet in my bedroom—
Perhaps you have one, too.

MY BROTHER PLAYS WITH CLOTHESPINS

My brother plays with clothespins.
He clips them in his hair,
On his fingertips and toes,
He clips them everywhere.

He attaches them to earlobes,
Elbows, knees, and lips.
I am actually amazed
At all the places he can clip.

Still I think it's rather strange
This is something he enjoys.
I've suggested that my parents go
And purchase him some toys!

IT'S HARD TO WAIT

It's hard to wait for Christmas.
It's hard to wait for spring.
And waiting for the school bus
Is not my favorite thing.

I hate to wait for birthdays.
Don't like to wait for summer.
And waiting for a parade to come
Can really be a bummer!

It's hard to wait for parties.
It's hard to wait for fall.
And waiting for the phone to ring
Can be the worst of all!

It's hard to wait for dinner,
When Daddy comes home late.
It seems when you're a little kid,
You always have to wait.

So when I say my bedtime prayers,
And I am on my knees,
I ask the Lord to send me
A lot of patience, please!

NOAH

I'm sure you've heard the story
Of Noah and the ark.
And how he worked so hard each day
From morning until dark.
The people mocked and teased him.
They laughed at him and said,
"That Noah sure is crazy!
He must be out of his head!"

But Noah kept on working.
He hammered and he sawed.
He built the ark from gopher wood
    While listening to his God.
        Now when the ark was finally done,
        His family got on board
        With two of every animal.
        And then it poured and poured.

The water flooded all the land,
And those who were unkind
Were sorry when the door was shut,
For they were left behind.
But Noah and his family
Were warm and safe and dry
For many months inside the ark,
As rain fell from the sky.

The Lord protected Noah,
His children, and his wife.
And Noah was rewarded
With a long and happy life.
Noah trusted in the Lord
And did what he was told.
He lived nine-hundred-fifty years—
Now that is very old!

LAURA LORRAINE

There once was a girl named Laura Lorraine.
Although very pretty,
she was terribly vain.
She snubbed all the kids
who were labeled as plain.
Laura Lorraine became such a pain!

Laura Lorraine thought she was cool,
the coolest girl
in the neighborhood school.
But she didn't obey
one single rule.
Laura Lorraine was a pitiful fool!

Laura Lorraine was told one day,
that she couldn't go out
on the playground to play.
All the kids shouted,
"Hooray! Hooray!"
Laura Lorraine didn't know what
to say.

Laura Lorraine had to stay inside.
She felt so bad
that she cried and she cried.
"No one likes me,"
poor Laura sighed.
Laura Lorraine was horrified!

Laura Lorraine then realized
that all the girls
and all the guys
only want to socialize
with those who don't antagonize.
Laura Lorraine became very wise.

Laura Lorraine soon changed her ways.
It took her three months
and twenty-four days,
but when she spoke
kind words of praise,
Laura's classmates were so amazed!

Laura Lorraine had lots of friends,
when her vain conceit
finally came to an end.
No longer did
her ways offend.
Laura Lorraine was a true-blue friend!

SUNDAY SCHOOL VERSE

I know my verse for Sunday School,
I've practiced all week long.
Today I'm going to say it,
There's no way I'll get it wrong.

I read it every morning,
And I said it every night.
I know my verse completely,
I will surely say it right.

I stood up very proudly
But nothing could be worse—
The words that I recited
Were the words to last week's verse!

THERE'S AN ALLIGATOR IN THE BATHTUB!

"Mother! Mother! Come quick! Come quick!
There's an alligator in the bathtub!
Mother! Mother! This is not a trick!
There's an alligator in the bathtub!"

My mother came and let out a sigh.
She said, "I've told you not to lie!
So go to your room and stay for awhile.
There's no alligator in here—
It's just a crocodile!"

NO, I DIDN'T

No, I didn't get ink on the chair.
My pen did that,
It's right over there.

No, I didn't track mud on the floor.
My shoes did that,
And they've done it before.

No, I didn't make a big mess.
My toys did that,
But they won't confess.

No, I didn't cut my own hair.
My scissors did that,
'Cause I wouldn't dare!

I always do the things I should.
  I'm never bad.
  I'm very good.

 So Mama, please don't punish me.
I'm innocent.
It's plain to see!

MY ADVENTUROUS GERBIL

I have an adventurous gerbil,
Who somehow escaped from his cage.
He scurried from his habitat,
And discovered a garden of sage.

He found a patch of parsley,
Rosemary, basil, and thyme.
And after he nibbled a smorgasbord,
He was truly feeling fine.

I don't know what happened exactly,
He's never been very verbal.
But one thing I know for certain,
He's a happy, herbal gerbil!

MARY ESTELLA

Mary Estella had an umbrella.
She carried it all the time.
On rainy days, on snowy days,
And when the sun would shine.

Mary Estella loved her umbrella.
She twirled it around and around,
Laughing, singing, and talking,
While strolling through the town.

Mary Estella had her umbrella
One very blustery day.
A gust of wind scooped her up,
And carried her away.

She floated over Africa,
And drifted over Spain.
She saw the sights of Italy,
And viewed the coast of Maine.

The gusty winds began to cease—
She slowly floated down.
Mary Estella and her umbrella
Returned to solid ground.

Mary Estella shut her umbrella
And said, "What a marvelous ride!
But next time the winds are gusty,
I think I'll stay inside!"

ROLLER COASTER

I'm on a roller coaster slowly chugging up a hill. Faster, faster flying down. Oh my goodness what a

I think I can tolerate this going up and down. Please, please let me get off so I can stand on solid ground!

QUESTIONS

Where does the sun go after it sets?
How do fish get caught in nets?

How does a rainbow form in the sky?
Why are the stars up so high?

How do birds know when to fly south?
Why do alligators have a big mouth?

Where do grizzlies hibernate?
Why do owls stay up late?

How does a caterpillar spin a cocoon?
How can a rocket shoot to the moon?

How do spiders spin a web?
Where do elephants go to bed?

What makes lightning, what makes thunder?
So many things just make me wonder.

What makes rain and what makes snow?
I'll go ask God, 'cause I don't know!

MY NEIGHBOR

My neighbor broke a windowpane.
My neighbor told a lie.
She yanks her sister's ponytail,
And makes her brother cry.

My neighbor's such a naughty girl.
My neighbor's really bad.
She talks back to her mother,
And she disobeys her dad.

My mom says not to play with her,
And I don't think I should.
It's just that when I'm with her,
She makes me look
So good!

CHICKEN SOUP

I have a stuffy-uffy nose.
"Chicken soup!" said Grandma.
I dropped a hammer on my toes.
"Chicken soup!" said Grandma.

My joints are sore, my muscles ache,
I ate too much banana cake,
I've been bitten by a rattlesnake.
"Chicken soup!" said Grandma.

I have a case of indigestion.
"Chicken soup!" said Grandma.
I need to cure severe depression.
"Chicken soup!" said Grandma.

I bumped my head and skinned my knee.
I've gotten stung by a honeybee.
Maybe I should have some tea.
"Chicken soup!" said Grandma.

What shall I buy at the grocery store?
"Chicken soup!" said Grandma.
What shall I eat forevermore?
"Chicken soup!" said Grandma.

I did just what my grandma said,
Each night before I went to bed—
I now have feathers on my head,
I scratch and claw at crumbs of bread.

My nose has changed into a beak.
I bawk and squawk instead of speak.
I even laid an egg last week!
"It's the chicken soup!" said Grandma.

THE REVOLVING DOOR

Once I went to a store
That had a revolving door.
It started to spin
But when I got in—
I came out where I was before.

SOMEDAY

Someday I'll clean my bedroom.
Someday I'll make my bed.
Someday I'll do the dishes
And make sure the fish are fed.

Someday I'll straighten my closet.
Someday I'll pick up my toys.
Someday I'll do my chores
Like other girls and boys.

Someday I'll be responsible,
Someday, somewhere, somehow—
We're going out for ice cream?
Okay, Mom, I'll do it now!

OFFICE CALL

As I walked to the office,
My knees began to shake.
My heart was beating faster,
And my head began to ache.

I wondered what I'd done
To get in such a mess.
I didn't steal or lie,
Or cheat on any test.

I didn't tease my classmates,
Or make the teacher cry.
I knew I was in trouble,
But I couldn't figure why.

My hands were getting sweaty,
My feet were turning numb.
I wondered if they'd called my mom,
To tell her what I'd done.

As I went inside the office,
I still didn't have a hunch.
Then the secretary said to me,
"Your mom dropped off your lunch!"

PRINCIPAL'S OFFICE

PAPER-CLIP CHAIN

I found a box of paper clips
And hooked them all together—
An appropriate activity
For cold, inclement weather.

The tiny silver paper clips
I hooked to one another.
"I have a brand-new hobby!"
I shouted to my mother.

It took me several hours
Before I finally quit.
I made a splendid ten-foot chain—
But now what do I do with it?

WHILE MOTHER WAS GONE

We should have made the beds.
We should have mowed the lawn.
We should have washed the dishes
While Mother was gone.

We should have got some work done,
But all we did was play.
We didn't do the things we should
While Mother was away.

I must admit we did have fun
Playing basketball,
And watching all those movies,
And going to the mall.

I really liked the soda pop
And pizza that we bought.
But pretty soon when Mother's home,
I hope we don't get caught.

I think I hear her coming.
I hope she won't be mad,
'Cause you're my all-time favorite
Baby-sitter, Dad!

WILMA WRONG AND
RICHARD RIGHT

Wilma Wrong loved Richard Right,
So they were married one autumn night.
They had some kids before too long
Who were partly Right and partly Wrong.

Sometimes they were very good,
And did the things that children should.
But sometimes they were awfully bad,
And made their parents very mad.

You might see them quietly play;
But then they'd start to disobey.
Often they would share their food;
But many times they acted rude.

Sometimes they would be polite;
Other times they'd scrap and fight.
And that is how they got along,
Being partly Right and partly Wrong.

THE SECRET

Come here—I have a secret
That I want to share with you.
It's a very special secret
And it's absolutely true!
I will tell you what the secret is:

GOD LOVES YOU!

But you have to share the secret,
And tell other people too!

ZACCHAEUS

The crowds began to gather 'round
as Jesus went walking
through the town.

Zacchaeus was too short to see—
so he climbed to the top
of a sycamore tree.

Now Zach was not a very nice guy.
He cheated his friends
and he told lots of lies.

But Jesus spied him up in the tree.
"Come down here," he said.
"Have some dinner with me."

They ate their dinner and talked for awhile.
Zacchaeus was changed—
and he started to smile.

He promised Jesus that he would be good
to all of the folks
in the neighborhood.

Zacchaeus changed his life that day,
and was glad that
Jesus came his way.

FREE AND A HALF

After I eat breffkiss,
I take a nice warm baff.
Mommy helps me tie my shoes,
I'm free years and a half.

I go outside to wide my bike,
I like to wun awound.
I like to look fo sticks and stones,
And find them on the gwound.

My buddy comes to pway wiff me.
We find my big wed ball.
We bounce and frow it back and foath.
We laugh until we fall.

My mommy calls me in the house
It's time fo me to eat—
Peter butter samiches
Are such a yummy tweet.

My mommy weads a stowy.
I cuddle on her lap.
I get a little sweepy
And then I take a nap.

YES, *I* DID IT

Yes, *I* did it.
I honestly did it.
I tripped on my lace
and broke
the vase.
There are bits
of glass
all over
the place.

Yes, *I* did it.
I honestly did it.
I poured the pop—
it wouldn't stop.
I'd better go
and get
the mop.

Yes, *I* did it.
I honestly did it.
I bumped the ladder
                and
                        spilled
                            the
                                paint.
I'm awkward and clumsy—
a little bit dumbsy,
but a liar is something
I ain't!

LAST

No matter where I seem to go,
I'm always last in line.
At church, at school, and summer camp,
It happens all the time.

I'm never first or second,
Or even in the middle.
It'd make me very happy,
If things could change a little.

I'm the one who's last in line,
It'll always be that way.
Oh, why couldn't I have been the one
Whose name begins with *A*?

WHAT IF?

What if bugs could talk?
What if fish could walk?
What if frogs had yellow hair?
Or snakes wore checkered underwear?

What do you think children would do,
If all the birds said "Moo, moo, moo"?
It'd surely be a different thing
If kangaroos could dance and sing.

Imagine all the noise and fuss
If sharks could ride the city bus!
And how would you begin to explain
A cat that drove a high-speed train?

Wouldn't it be cool, cool, cool
If elephants taught grammar school?
And wouldn't it be really neat
If jellyfish had purple feet?

But what if dogs laid eggs?
And what if worms had legs?
What if skunks were tall?
Or geese played basketball?

What if alligators
Were waitresses and waiters?
Wouldn't it be funny
To see a polka-dot bunny?

I certainly would laugh
To see a striped giraffe.
But surely I would cry
If cows and pigs could fly.

We're better off by far
With things the way they are!

THERE'S A PARROT ON MY SHOULDER

There's a parrot on my shoulder
And I wonder why he's here.
His claws are long and pointed
And he nibbles on my ear.

He repeats and he repeats
Almost every word I say.
I don't know where he came from,
But I wish he'd go away.

I cannot kick my soccer ball,
I cannot take a shower.
He stays right on my shoulder
Every minute of the hour.

My friends no longer play with me.
I cannot go to church.
I don't know why he's chosen
My shoulder for his perch.

Yes, it's very inconvenient
With this parrot on my shoulder.
The only thing that I can do
Is sit here and grow older.

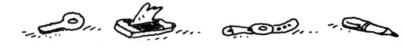

I LOST MY QUARTER

I lost my quarter, I lost my gum.
I lost my candy, it wasn't fun.
I lost my tissue, I lost my key.
Oh, why do these things
Always happen to me?

I lost my paper, I lost my pen.
I lost my dime, here I go again.
I lost my watch and my little
   toy rocket.
Maybe I'll stitch up
The hole in my pocket!

BREAD AND FISH

Once there was a fine young lad.
Some bread and fish were all he had.
Then Jesus asked if he would share
His lunch with all the people there.

The lad gave Jesus all his lunch,
And wondered how he'd feed this bunch.
For there were thousands to be fed
With two small fish
And a loaf of bread.

Then Jesus took the lunch and prayed.
The people all sat down and stayed.
The fine young lad was quite surprised
As food appeared before his eyes.

The bread and fish were passed around
And extra food fell on the ground.
The people talked and munched and crunched,
As they enjoyed the tasty lunch.

The fine young lad found out that day
What happens when we share and pray.
For all the people there were fed,
With his two small fish
And a loaf of bread.

SATURDAY

Hooray! Today is Saturday,
my favorite day
to go out and play.
Maybe today I'll ride my bike
or call a friend
and go for a hike.
Perhaps I'll play some basketball
or maybe later
I'll go to the mall.

But now that I'm sitting up in bed,
my stomach hurts,
and so does my head.
My face is hot, my hands are cold.
I've got the flu—
so I am told.

So I didn't go out to ride my bike,
or call a friend,
or go for a hike.
I didn't play any basketball
and I didn't take a trip to the mall.

Here is what I did instead:
I STAYED IN BED!

OUR BRIGHT AND COLORFUL WORLD

Blue is the color God put in the sky,
A robin's egg, and blueberry pie.
Red is the color of sweet-smelling roses,
Strawberry jam, and frost-bitten noses.
Green is the color of soft summer leaves,
Velvety grass, and stains on my knees.
The bright yellow sun feels warm on my skin.
Sweet yellow corn gets all over my chin.
Violets are purple, and so is a plum.

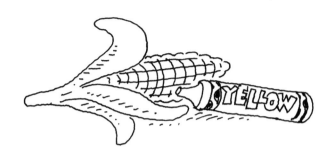

My favorite purple is grape bubble gum.
Pumpkins are orange, and tangerines, too.
I like drinking orange juice, how about you?
God made the elephant wrinkled and gray.
Gray are the clouds on a cold winter day.
Squirrels and beavers and bears can be brown.
Brown is the color way down in the ground.
When I see a rainbow with colors so bright,
I'm happy the world is not black and white!

WORMS FOR SALE

WORMS FOR SALE!
WORMS FOR SALE!
FIFTY CENTS A WORM.
FAT AND ROUND,
DON'T MAKE A SOUND,
SOME DON'T EVEN SQUIRM!

WORMS FOR SALE!
WORMS FOR SALE!
WORMS FOR JUST A QUARTER.
SKINNY RED ONES,
NOT-QUITE-DEAD ONES,
PLACE A SPECIAL ORDER.

Worms for sale.
Worms for sale.
How about a nickle?
A tasty dish
For any fish—
Works better than a pickle!

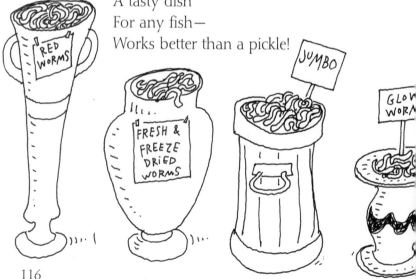

worms for sale
worms for sale
only cost a penny
i've got a lot—
get 'em while they're hot
'cause soon I won't have any.

FREE WORMS!
FREE WORMS!
DON'T EVEN NEED A DIME!

But just the same,
No one came.
So all these worms are mine.

TYLER TIM

My name is Tyler Tim.
My brother and I are twins.
Sometimes I can't remember
If I'm me or if I'm him.

We both have curly hair.
We're totally alike.
Except that my name's Tyler,
And my brother's name is Mike.

JONAH

Jonah was a prophet.
God told him what to say,
But he didn't like the message
So he tried to run away.
He got on board a ship
That headed out to sea,
But soon a storm arose—
It was windy as could be.

Everyone was frightened.
They thought that they would die.
Then Jonah told the people,
"I'm the reason why
The waves and winds are very fierce,
So throw me overboard.
I've been a sinful prophet
For I've disobeyed the Lord."

The people threw him off the ship
Just as Jonah said.
A fish came by and swallowed him,
But Jonah wasn't dead.
He lived for days inside the fish,
He prayed and prayed and prayed.
So God gave him a second chance—
And this time he obeyed!

CLEANING MY DESK

It's the last day of school,
and I'm cleaning my desk.
I've got dozens of pencils
and leftover tests.

Let's see—
twenty erasers,
thirty-five pens,
and forty-six notes
from my very best friends.

A compass, a ruler,
a protractor too,
a package of markers,
a bottle of glue.

Gum wrappers, candy bars,
suckers galore—
out of my desk
and onto the floor.

A moldy old sandwich—
tuna and rye,
some stale jelly beans
and a single french fry.

Oh, *there's* my math book,
my science book too,
and an English assignment
that's way overdue.

Key chains and jewelry,
my eyeglasses case—
so many items
in such a small place!

As I examine
the things that are here,
I have to admit—
it was quite a good year!

THE VISITOR

The preacher was preaching his sermon,
He had a message to tell.
But the audience was squirmin',
And they could not listen well.

The little girls were squealing—
Tiny, whispery squeals.
They pointed their toes to the ceiling
And lifted up their heels.

The boys began to chatter
As quietly as they could,
For something was the matter,
And they knew it wasn't good!

The men and women looked around
At others in the pew.
Trying not to make a sound
Was difficult to do.

Then someone finally shouted,
"Hey, look! There goes a mouse!"
The preacher answered,
"That's okay.
He's welcome in God's house!"

TOO EARLY

It's much too early to go to bed.
Let's read my favorite books instead.
Hey! Maybe we can bake a cake,
Or go outside and catch a snake.

I think I need to do my math,
Or take another bubble bath.
Maybe we can sit and talk,
Or take the puppy for a walk.

I'm thirsty and I need a drink.
It's much too early, don't you think?
Look outside—it's barely dark!
Tell me the story of Noah's ark.

I have to put my toys away,
And don't you think that we should pray?
It's much too early to say good night.
Hey wait! Who just turned out the light?

MAYBE

Maybe if I had a bike,
I'd go and visit Uncle Mike.

Maybe if I owned a car,
I'd pack my bags and travel far.

Maybe if I had a bus,
I'd drive it to Los Angeles.

Maybe if I owned a train,
I'd ride it all the way to Maine.

Maybe if I had a ship,
I'd sail away and take a trip.

Maybe if I had a plane,
I'd fly it all the way to Spain.

But all I have is my two feet,
So I'll just walk across the street.

DON'T FORGET TO SAY YOUR PRAYERS

Dear God, I know you're by my side
No matter where I go.
And I should never be afraid,
My mama told me so.

But when it's time to go to bed
And Dad turns out the light,
It makes me very glad to know
That you stay up all night.

INDEX